GW00402133

WHAT IS LOVE?

Also by Giles Andreae

PURPLE RONNIE'S BOOK OF LOVE
PURPLE RONNIE'S GUIDE TO LIFE
THE SMASHING WORLD OF PURPLE RONNIE
PURPLE RONNIE'S STAR SIGNS

WHAT IS LOVE?

Giles Andreae

Illustrations by
Janet Cronin

Hodder & Stoughton
LONDON SYDNEY AUCKLAND

To my parents
And to Sam

First published in great Britain in 1994 by Hodder & Stoughton
A division of Hodder Headline PLC
10 9 8 7 6 5 4 3 2 1

ISBN 0 340 62840 5
Printed and bound in Great Britain for
Hodder and Stoughton Ltd
A division of Hodder Headline PLC
338 Euston Road
London NW1 3BH
by Mackays of Chatham PLC

Contents

WHAT IS LOVE?

I love dancing

what a lovely hairstyle

Without Love

One thing is for sure...

When we see someone who's got it
there's no mistaking it

When people have love we can feel the buzz

With Love

They affect everything around them.

Love is an attitude
towards the world

Love is what stops us from feeling alone.
It unites us with others, with ourselves and
with life.

Love is what makes people grow inside.

DO WE NEED LOVE?

Yes we do.

We need to
receive love
in order
to grow...

...and we need to
give love in order to
feel alive.

If we do not give and receive love
all the time...

...we cut ourselves off from life.

HOW DO WE GET LOVE?

Is it something that drops on us from out of the blue?

Is it something that pours itself into us?

Is it something that we fall into when we're not looking?

Or is it something that's bursting to get out of us...

...if only the right person would come along and free it?

If it were any of these, how sad the world would be if love just by accident failed to drop, pour, fall or burst into us.

There would be millions of nice, good, beautiful and worthy people who just never managed to get any love.

THE SECRET OF LOVE

People often think that they would find true love
if only they could find the right
person to love…

…and the right person to love them

But love is not like shopping.

Love is not something
that <u>happens to you</u>...

Love is something
that <u>you make happen</u>.

HOW DOES LOVE WORK?

Love begins with giving.

And the amazing thing about it is...
the more love you give...

...the more love you get back.

If I give you a chocolate
it makes <u>me</u> happy
because I know you
like chocolates...

...and it makes <u>you</u>
happy because it's
delicious and because
I smile when you take it.

mmm thanks

Now we are both
smiling you give
me one of your
chocolates to
make us even
happier.

Soon we will both be stuffed full of chocolates and laughing out loud with happiness.

Love, unlike chocolates, does not run out
or make you fat.

If you practise love every day you will soon become so good at it...

...that you will bring to life everything around you.

FALLING IN LOVE

I'm not falling in love...

...I'm rising

Scientists say that falling in love happens when two people have the right mixture of chemicals for each other.

But falling in love hasn't got much to do with science.

Falling in love
happens when
you take some
love…

…mix it with attraction

Aim it at
one person…

…and FIRE!

WHAT YOU FEEL WHEN YOU FALL IN LOVE...

Everything is fun. Everything is worth doing. Every little thing makes me buzz with happiness because now I have you.

I am naked and bare in front of you and I want to share everything about myself with you.

We have such a special way of understanding each other. Nobody has ever felt this way before.

I want to surprise you, thrill you, indulge you...

...and show you what an amazing person I am to have fallen in love with.

You are the best
person I have ever
made love with
ever.

You are the most incredible person in the
Universe. Even your little habits are fantastic.

The world is full of wonders. Anything is possible. Everything seems new. I feel like a child again.

But after a while the ecstasy of falling in love begins to fade

Stop picking your nose!
get your hands out of your pockets!
don't make nasty smells!
pick up your clothes!

and the thrill of your newness to each other wears off.

you don't fancy me anymore
you're only interested in your own things
you're always getting at me
you never sa
you love m
anymore

It is only when you
stop falling in love...

...and start
being in love...

...that you can really
begin to love each
other fully.

DOES LOVE LAST FOR EVER?

Loving someone fully means doing things rather than feeling things...

...and to make love last for ever there are lots of things which you must do.

Trust

You can only grow in love together if you have the freedom to <u>choose</u> to love each other.

Trust is what gives you the freedom to love.

Respect

All sorts of different bits and pieces go into making up a person.

Respect means loving all the different bits and pieces...

...and not just the ones that you find most attractive.

Respect is what gives you the confidence
to become yourself.

Effort

To be good at anything takes a
lot of work, time and practice.

Effort means making love -
the most important thing
in your life.

Communication

Love means putting time aside to really listen.

Learning new things about each other all the time is what keeps love alive.

Commitment

Some people think they will always find
something better round the corner...

...but there are always more corners
to look round.

Commitment is what gives you
the confidence to love more fully.

People who are frightened of commitment...

...are frightened of love.

Support

People who do not give and receive support
never get better at anything…

…except hurting each other.

But people who support each other
can achieve miracles.

LIVING IN LOVE

But love is not
just about two
people loving
each other

It is about the way we treat everyone
in our lives every day.

Once we understand that love is what
holds the world together...

...then we can learn to become Loving People.

Some people are
born to love…

…others find
loving difficult.

But everyone can become a Loving Person
if they really try.

LOVING PEOPLE

Loving People...

Work at Love

A lot of people know that love is important...

...but they would rather spend their time doing other things.

Loving people know that love is the most important thing in the world

and that the more you put into love...

...the more you get out of it.

Loving People...

Love You as You Are

Some people want to change others
to adapt them to their own needs.

But Loving People know that you can only be happy when you are allowed to be the person who you already are.

Loving People...

Don't Put Values on Their Friendships

People who are always judging their friends
don't end up with any friends at all.

Loving People know
that whatever happens...

...friends should remain friends for ever.

Loving People...

Are Not Afraid of Taking Risks

People who spend all their time avoiding risks...

...are really avoiding life.

Loving People know they will never regret the things they do, but only the things they don't do

and that only if you risk things can you get the most out of life.

Loving People...

Love Everyone

Some people
think you can
only love one
person at a
time

you're the
only one for
me sweetypie

and some people
only love others
who serve a purpose.

But Loving People's love
gets into everyone...

...and everything.

Loving People...

Mean What They Say

Some people only say "I love you" to get what they want

When Loving People say "I love you" you can see they mean it.

And Say What
They Mean

Some people are afraid
to say what they want
to say

But Loving People know
that great things can
only happen...

...when you say what you're really feeling
inside.

Loving People...

Are Awake to the World

People who walk around with their heads in the air never notice anything and never learn anything.

Loving People know that love means...

...constantly learning about life

A FINAL WORD

Everyone is born with beauty inside them...

...and LOVE is what brings the inside beauty out.